DISNEY · PIXAR

THE INCREDIBLES

THE INCREDI-FILES

Written by
John Edwards

rhcbooks.com

ISBN 978-0-7364-3860-5

Printed in the United States of America

10 9 8 7 6 5 4 3 2 1

Random House New York

A message from Winston Deavor,
Co-founder and CEO, DevTech

Sometimes Even Supers Need Heroes

From Municiberg to New Urbem, it's the dawn of a new day.

But as the recent Omnidroid attack and the Underminer incident show,
it's still a day that needs saving.

And because it does, I am putting the considerable resources of the
company I created, Deavor Industries, behind the Deavor Initiative
to repeal the Super Relocation Program (SRP).

It's time for Supers to suit up, put their masks back on, and come out
of hiding.

This dossier encompasses all the information we've collected in our effort
to bring Supers back, better and stronger than ever before, to fight crime.

Winston Deavor

DEVTECH

Deavor Initiative

CONFIDENTIAL

Mission: Repeal the Super Relocation Program
Spearhead movement to help bring Supers back to the forefront.
The Deavor Initiative will upgrade each Super's tech to match his or her
public image with a three-phase strategy.

STRATEGY OVERVIEW

Phase One
- Introduce the repeal of the Super Relocation Program
- Recruit A-level Supers (the most famous ones)
- Provide equipment upgrades as needed
- Accomplish small, single-hero missions to build
  buzz and public trust

Phase Two
- Recruit B-level Supers (the least famous ones)
- Bigger missions
- More coverage: talk shows, public appearances,
  and maybe product endorsements?

Phase Three
- Audition Supers for teams
- Acquire agents and managers for all Supers
- Full rollout of the repeal of the Super Relocation Program

Media, media, media!
—WD

*Super mall openings
would be a
no-brainer, eh?
—WD*

Note to Legal: Can we copyright "Herollout"? —WD
Please stop creating new words. —ED

Background on the
Super Relocation Program (SRP)

Once upon a time, Supers were on every magazine cover and every talk show. They were everywhere we needed them to be. Super villains? No problem. Natural disasters? Piece of cake. Maniacal robots? Easy-peasy.

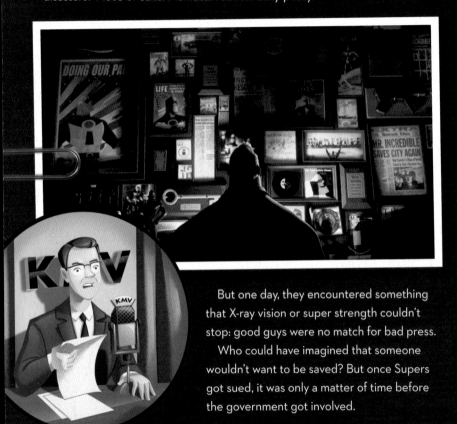

But one day, they encountered something that X-ray vision or super strength couldn't stop: good guys were no match for bad press.

Who could have imagined that someone wouldn't want to be saved? But once Supers got sued, it was only a matter of time before the government got involved.

The Super Relocation Program (SRP) was created to keep the Supers safe. But in return for dismissing lawsuits, the heroes had to stop being super. That meant they had to take off their capes and masks for good and assume new identities as ordinary, mild-mannered civilians.

is Tribune DAILY 5°
EDITION

DIBLE
AT SE

EXTRA

9 A.M. FINAL Newtropolis Tribune 9 A.M. FINAL

VOL. XIV

MONDAY, SEPTEMBER 19TH, 2005

DAILY 5 CENTS

MISTER INCREDIBLE
RETIRES

The Red Menace Captain Capitalist Collide in the skies

New Spandex Modern Miracle of Science

Superhero Sightings at Record Low

Safer or more at risk?

Superhero Bids Farewell in Last Public Appearance

Hero Insurance Rates Skyrocket

WITH SOME DEEP DIGGING, WE HAVE OBTAINED COPIES OF NSA DOCUMENTS. THOSE COPIES ARE INCLUDED THROUGHOUT THIS FILE.

MEMO
To: New Recruits
From: R. Dicker
Re: National Supers Agency

National Supers Agency (NSA) is a top-secret agency designed to protect the identities of those extraordinary heroes known as Supers, who once kept the populace safe.

Unfortunately, the Supers' daring acts of heroism sometimes resulted in accidents. By the time the NSA intervened, the Supers were facing lawsuits, bankruptcy, and public humiliation. The global backlash against their heroic acts put their very lives in danger.

For the past fifteen years, we at the NSA and our agents have devoted ourselves to keeping the Supers safe. We initiate and support their relocations and new identities.

Enclosed in this file are mementos, artifacts, and documents that tell the official history of the NSA and the Supers. Remember, these files are TOP-SECRET and must be kept clean of all identifying fingerprints and traces of DNA! Good luck—and be careful!

R. Dicker

CO

NOTE: Recently, Supers have been permitted a few heroic acts. Be alert—we must still protect their undercover identities, while occasionally letting them save the populace!

Immediate surveillance recommended on <u>Frozone</u> and <u>Mr. Incredible</u>

It all started with this guy.

Family of five Supers—
the Incredibles
Matching suits designed by Edna Mode

COPY

★ CONFIDENTIAL ★

THE SUPER RELOCATION PROGRAM (SRP)

Who: Agents who have sworn to protect Supers at all costs.

What: An NSA-funded program established to relocate Supers and give them new identities for their own protection.

Where: Wherever we need to go to complete our mission.

How: By whatever means necessary.

Why: Out of honor and respect for their noble deeds and former heroics.

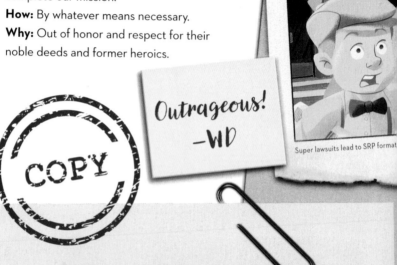

MIGHTY MENACE!

Super lawsuits lead to SRP format

COPY

Outrageous!
—WD

SRP Pledge

As an agent of the Super Relocation Program, I promise to do my best to:

· Relocate Supers
· Keep Supers' identities hidden
· Protect Supers from harm

CONFIDENTIAL

R. Dicker

Government Forms "Secret" Program to Protect Supers

Photo by: Michael Lewis

Secret source never identified. Internal government leak suspected.

By Mark Ramsey

In an unprecedented move, the government issued a top-secret internal memo stating that it would start a relocation program to hide and protect the Supers of the world. "Someone's gotta do something," our secret source told us. "These Supers are being sued for everything. One lady complained that her jar of mayonnaise was cracked by an overly zealous Super kid carrying her groceries to her car. She claimed it cost her $1.35, plus a million in emotional stress."

Some Supers require extra attention. Case study: Bob Parr. He cannot let go of the past.

Attention, all SRP agents:

Secret identities sometimes change on a daily basis. Refer to Relocation Handbook for more classified info.

COPY

The Supers' Heyday

Before the Supers went undercover, they were adored by the populace. It was a time when everyone felt proud to show their respect for their heroes.

This file contains samples of objects that Super fans collected.

The Supers were commonly featured in the pages of newspapers and magazines, kids wore imitation Super masks, and fan buttons were very popular.

Unfortunately, some fans took their adoration too far. Reference: Syndrome file.

The Super Years

Mr. Incredible and Frozone at a charity event.

CONFIDENTIAL

COPY

I'm a BIG Fan of Mr. Incredible!

Super memorabilia brings big $ these days.

SUPER OF THE YEAR

Heroes spent a lot of time—perhaps too much time—in the public eye.

SPRING
Vol. 1 Issue 1

$1.25

An Incredible Fall for One of Our Best Heroes

Love
this pic!
—ED

Vol. 20   Issue 1

$1.75

Overly zealous fan Buddy spotted as wannabe sidekick Incrediboy.

THE INCREDIBILE

The Most "Super" Vehicle Ever?

Some of the newer agents may not remember the early years of the SRP. Times were tough for the Supers, and there were some outrageous and illegitimate lawsuits. The Supers couldn't seem to win favor even from the very citizens they saved!

MEMO

To: New Recruits

From: R. Dicker

Re: Supers' Undercover Operations

- Monitor Supers 24/7. Prevent all future rescue attempts.
- Assign new names, new homes, and new jobs to Supers.
- Contact R. Dicker if Supers are summoned to court.

★ CONFIDENTIAL ★

Vol. 15   Issue 3

LEGAL JOURNAL

Subject identified as Oliver Sansweet. He didn't want to be saved.
—ED

Sansweet Awarded Record Payment in **Super Lawsuit!**

HIGHER COURT
Pledges to Uphold Ruling!

Child Awarded $1 Million in Stuffed Bear Incident

Some particularly embarrassing incidents only worsened the Supers' status in their communities.

So-called hero offers to replace burnt teddy bear.

Photo by: Jacob Jordy

By G. Lizer

Super-Big Mistake

A top Super was ordered to pay a three-year-old girl $1 million. Apparently the Super raced into the little girl's burning house and saved her family, but thought the little girl's favorite stuffed bear wasn't important. Dozens of witnesses testified about the emotional distress inflicted on the child. Reports of public outrage have forced the Super to go into hiding. Who do these Supers think they are?

Due to the unfortunate reactions of some ungrateful people, the Supers faced a hard fall. SRP agents must be aware of the difficult changes our heroes had to make when they went undercover, never to use their Super powers again.

The Sansweet case spurred a media frenzy.

$$$

SUPERS
NO MORE
INCREDIBLE

DEVTECH

SUPER
PERSONNEL

From: Evelyn
To: Winston

Subject: Super Personnel

I'm still not convinced we even need the Deavor Initiative, but if it's going to succeed, we've got to pick the right Super or (Supers) to start with. We'll need to review known Supers, evaluate their strengths and weaknesses, then focus-test the top candidates.

I suggest we look at the Incredibles: they have strong franchise possibilities, are a recognized brand, and appeal to all demographics (and we know where to find them). Attached are their profiles. I've also included some other possible candidates.

—WD

Yes! The family angle sells!
—ED

At the end of the golden age of the Supers, Mr. Incredible and his wife, Elastigirl, went underground as part of the Super Relocation Program. They continue to live undercover as Bob and Helen Parr, a typical suburban couple with three children, a sunny ranch house, and an average family car.

COPY

Family squabbles suspicious to neighbors. Heavy curtains needed ASAP!

NOTE TO FILE

The Parrs have had trouble containing their powers in the past. They've been relocated several times. See enclosed evidence.

★ CONFIDENTIAL ★

WARNING: Monitor closely. If any neighbor should look in the window during a family argument like this, the Parrs' undercover status would be ruined.

Official SRP Address Book
CONFIDENTIAL MATERIAL INTERNAL USE ONLY!

Name   Robert & Helen Parr
        Violet, Dash & Jack-Jack

Address   Relocation #1
           ~~1107 Madison Ave~~
           ~~Pleasant Hill, CA~~

Address   Relocation #2
           ~~210 McKenzie Circle~~
           ~~Moraga, CA 94556~~

Address   Relocation #3
           ~~157 Avery Way~~
           ~~Tucson, CA 94556~~

Address

Address

Address

Address

★ CONFIDENTIAL ★

Note: Discuss with Helen! She should not be stretching in any photos.
—ED

Rubble from incident 050474 spotted on Bob's jacket. He was not caught by the police, but he was caught by Helen.

COPY

Mr. Incredible

ALIAS:
Robert "Bob" Parr

STRENGTHS:
Super strength
Experienced as an "old days" hero
Dedicated family man

WEAKNESSES:
Big ego
Works alone

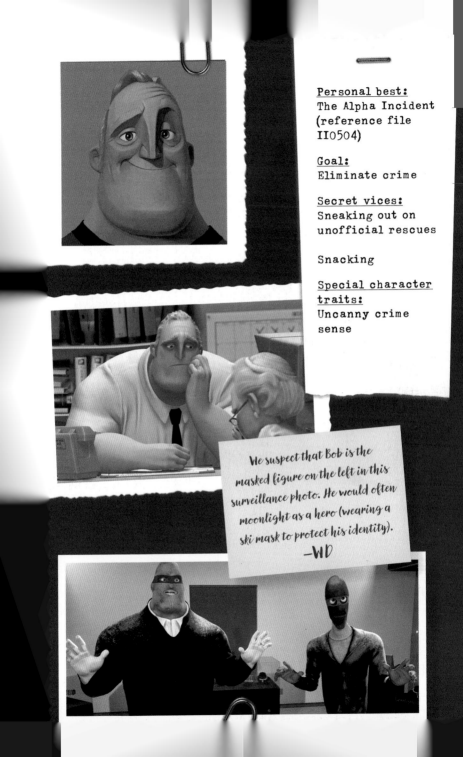

Personal best:
The Alpha Incident
(reference file
II0504)

Goal:
Eliminate crime

Secret vices:
Sneaking out on
unofficial rescues

Snacking

Special character traits:
Uncanny crime
sense

We suspect that Bob is the masked figure on the left in this surveillance photo. He would often moonlight as a hero (wearing a ski mask to protect his identity).

—WD

MR. INCREDIBLE

New Mr. Incredible fan memorabilia spotted at recent comic-book convention.

COPY

Notification of Termination
Insuricare, Inc.

You're FIRED! Robert Parr

This is to inform you that we will no longer require your services.

Note to file

Bob was offered one last relocation, but he refused.

★ CONFIDENTIAL ★

Mr. Incredible
Voice Recording
For voice-matching purposes only.
CONFIDENTIAL MATERIAL
Internal use only—property of SRP

1.44 MB

The Super Years

On the day depicted, Mr. Incredible:

1. Rescued a cat and stopped bank robbers with a tree (later replanted by said hero).
2. Saved a jumper.
3. Removed a live bomb.
4. Stopped a train from plunging to disaster.

Jumper and train passengers started lawsuits.

The Undercover Years

Contact Bob immediately. Anyone with a good telescope can catch him during one of his Super workouts.

A Super New Era

THINGS TO DO:

1. Mow lawn
2. Watch football
3. Pick up dry cleaning
4. Treadmill
5. Follow up Bomb Voyage incident

Note: Bomb Voyage spotted recently at a French brasserie downtown. —WD

Remember the Elasticycle? Let's get R&D working on an upgrade. Can we build a motorcycle that stretches, too?
—WD

Elastigirl

ALIAS:
Helen Parr

STRENGTHS:
Full-body elasticity
Licensed pilot
Uncanny crime sense

WEAKNESS:
Freezing temperatures

Most embarrassing moment:
Waiting for her groom at the altar

Greatest achievements:
Violet, Dash, and Jack-Jack

Secret vices:
Reaching into the kitchen freezer for ice cream in bed (without getting out of bed)

Special talents:
Waking the kids for school while making breakfast, feeding Jack-Jack, doing the laundry, and taking out the trash

Her flexibility and low collateral-damage-to-rescue ratio makes her ideal for the Deavor Initiative.
—WD

Marrying Mr. Incredible was more than the ultimate Super team-up; it was the start of Elastigirl's greatest adventure.

ELASTIGIRL

Elastigirl continues
to blend well with
the community.
—ED

COPY

CARPOOL SCHEDULE

MONDAY	Helen Parr	Jacob, Jordyn, Kai, Taidan, and Dash
TUESDAY	Beth Giles	Erin, Lucy, Devin, Ben, Taidan, and Dash
WEDNESDAY	Dovie Ramsey	Madison, Mackenzie, Taidan, and Dash

★ CONFIDENTIAL

Elastigirl
Voice Recording
For voice-matching purposes only.
**CONFIDENTIAL
MATERIAL**
Internal use only—property of SRP

1.44 MB

The Super Years

Elastigirl was one of the most intelligent Supers during the glory days. Her choice of Mr. Incredible as a husband was a match made in Super heaven. (This historic photo shows Elastigirl's original Supersuit. It also shows her old hairstyle, for the record.)

★ CONFIDENTIAL ★

The Undercover Years

The wedding day of Bob & Helen

Experience proves
that we can always
rely on Helen Parr
to maintain her
cover.

almost

A Super New Era

Helen is a good influence on Bob. She's successfully balanced being a Super and an undercover mom.

Stretch That Budget with These Super Shopping Tips

A special article by Elastigirl

Ever feel as if you need to become a Super in order to stretch your household budget? Shopping for a Super-active family calls for strategic planning and a flexible mind. For instance, if your list calls for one carton of double-fudge chocolate chip ice cream, and triple-fudge mint brownie is on sale at the market in th

Violet

ALIAS:
Violet "Vi" Parr

STRENGTHS:
Invisibility
Can generate force fields

WEAKNESSES:
Adolescence
Sibling rivalry (see Dash)
Inexperience

SRP red flags:
Likes to hide
(sometimes we
can't find her!)

Secret wishes:
Go out with
classmate
named Tony

Marry Tony

Be normal

Greatest
achievement:
Helping her family
save Metroville

Note: Violet's been seeing a lot of Tony Rydinger.

Along with discovering her powers, Violet is discovering BOYS.

Tony works at the Happy Platter.
After extensive observation, we've concluded that:

1. Tony has no observable powers—but is described by Vi as "dreamy."
2. This family-style eatery is clean and affordable.
3. The cheesy buffalo wings platter is an excellent choice.

VIOLET

MOM... DAD...

Violet

Diary entries need to be monitored. Destroy evidence regarding family's Super powers.

The Undercover Years

dear diary   TONY + VIOLET

Some days I wish I could just put all this Super stuff behind me and be normal. My family is too weird: Dad goes out all night and returns with torn shirts and rubble on his shoulder. (Like we don't know you've been secretly trying to save people, Dad!) When I'm at home with my friends, it's like one minute Dash is locked out of my room and the next minute he's looking in the window! Mom stretches herself too much. It's really embarrassing. I totally saw her underwear tonight when she reached for

A Super New Era

Vi came out of her shell (but luckily not out of her force field!) to help defeat the Omnidroid. This Super kid has lots of potential.

Evidence of underground Violet memorabilia discovered after high school dance. Super popularity is growing.
—WD

CONFIDENTIAL

COPY

NOTE TO FILE
How to keep track of a kid with the power to turn invisible? Check SRP handbook.

Violet's intelligence adds to her Super powers. This surveillance photo shows her hacking into Syndrome's computer.

From: Winston

To: Evelyn

Subject: Faster than the speed of . . . ?

Just how fast is Dash, anyway? He can run on water and he's only 10?!?

Please research!
—WD

Velocity = distance / time

Distance from Dash's desk to teacher's desk = 23 feet (46 feet round-trip)

To avoid being seen on camera, Dash would have to run faster than the speed of the film, which is 29.97 frames per second, or .066 feet per second.

46 / .066 = 475 mph

Note: This is not necessarily Dash's top speed. Plus as he gets older, it is very likely that his top speed will increase. In other words, by the time he can drive, Dash may be able to break the sound barrier . . . on foot!

—ED

Dash

ALIAS:
Dashiell Robert Parr

STRENGTH:
Super speed

WEAKNESSES:
Impulse control
Sibling rivalry (see Violet)

From: Evelyn
To: Winston

Subject: Dash's speed

Dash has yet to be properly tested, but based on closed-circuit footage and data we have, I've devised the following calculation. First, to avoid sinking, Dash would have to maintain a speed of 85 mph. By comparison, the world's fastest mammal (other than Dash), the cheetah, only reaches a maximum speed of 75 mph.

Since I know you prefer pictures, I included the following comparison chart:

—ED

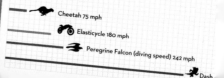

Cheetah 75 mph
Elasticycle 180 mph
Peregrine Falcon (diving speed) 242 mph
Dash

DASH

CONFIDENTIAL

Dash Undercover

Note to file

Put a surveillance team on track coach. He's getting suspicious about all the second-place finishes. Consider having Dash come in third at next race.

—ED

Watch the daydreaming at school! When Dash is bored, trouble follows.

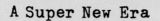

A Super New Era

Dash has truly found his balance. He looks to his parents for help and stays out of trouble by venting just enough of his Super energy running track.

Photo taken by Syndrome's surveillance shows Dash first discovering the full potential of his powers. This kid can run on water!

COPY

Only SRP-issue, super-high-speed film can capture Dash's speed.

Dash has really shown his stuff. If not for this boy's speed, Syndrome might be ruling the world.

CONFIDENTIAL

RED FLAG!!!

Mr. Kropp is asking too many questions. Put under immediate surveillance!

Dear Mr. and Mrs. Parr, Mr. Kropp is requesting a parent-teacher conference regarding your son Dash. Please call the school office to set up an appointment.

Jack-Jack

ALIAS:
Jack-Jack Parr

STRENGTHS (known):
A known polymorph
Mimicry
Dimensional teleportation
Control of fire
Levitation
Self-cloning
Monstrous tendencies
Spontaneous combustion
Telekinesis
Self-detonation

WEAKNESSES:
Unknown

FAVORITE FOODS:
Cookies (Num-Nums)
Mashed carrots
Milk

NOTE: Jack-Jack's
powers are coming
in faster than his
baby teeth and are
still unpredictable.
However, different
styles of music
helps soothe the
savage baby.
(See Tech Subject:
the Jack-Jack
Tracker.)

Birth Certificate

This is to Certify that

Jack-Jack Parr

oz. was born

JACK-JACK: 031104

JACK-JACK

★ CONFIDENTIAL ★

COPY

Who leaked all this info? (Note to self: Check whether all this is true.)

Place full-time watch on the babysitter—she saw a lot of Jack-Jack.
—ED

At first, little Jack-Jack posed no threat to the undercover status of the Parr family. He was just a cute baby with no Super powers. But now SRP is on high alert. All agents should keep an eye on this kid.

Helen has kept Jack-Jack under control up till now—but she will need help soon! Teen years could prove dangerous.

ALERT!
This cute baby face hides strange powers.
(NOTE TO SELF:
Keep an eye on Jack-Jack—and lollipops handy!)

Jack-Jack may possess more powers than already identified. Powers noticed thus far: can transform into fire, metal, and some sort of mini monster.

(actual size at birth)

CONFIDENTIAL

COPY

From: Evelyn
To: Winston

Subject: Super Childcare

All babies have meltdowns, but most children don't have the potential to level city blocks. That's why I had our on-site childcare center and some of the engineers at DevTech work up the Caregiver. It's the first of its kind—a diaper kit exclusively for Supers!

Many Supers have utility belts, and Jack-Jack is no exception. But this equipment is for his babysitter. Instead of grappling hooks and sonic phasers, baby Jack-Jack's kit looks a little different:

Jack-Jack Tracker

Bib

Diaper

Powder

THE CAREGIVER

DEVTECH

To Do: Contact Deavor Marketing Dept.
Subject: Product endorsement opportunities

Jack-Jack as the new face of
all kinds of Num-Nums?
—WD

DEVTECH

ALLIES

When the Supers were forced into retirement, Lucius was able to acclimate more easily than most. This may be in part thanks to his clothing line (debuting this winter) and a career in the music industry.

Some give credit to his wife, Honey, who knows how to chill him out (and periodically hides his Supersuit).

Plus, with his extremely low save-to-damage ratio, he's a hot pick for the Deavor Initiative. All the hero with none of the headache.

Frozone

ALIAS:
Lucius Best

STRENGTHS:
Can generate ice from moisture
Master speed skater on ice pathways he creates

WEAKNESS:
Requires moisture in order to create ice

Reputation
about town:
Super cool

Super relationships:
Mr. Incredible's
best friend

Married to Honey

Best save:
Putting the freeze
on a thousand-acre
wildfire

Secret wish:
To own a Super
car like the
Incredibile

His visor serves a dual purpose of preventing both snow blindness and the discovery of his true identity.

Frozone's boots are a real marvel. They adapt to various ice conditions and can convert into skates, skis, snowboards, etc., as needed.

FROZONE

Maintained his professional ethics even when undercover. Refused to try out for winter sports events.
—WD

CONFIDENTIAL ★

A Super New Era

After helping conquer Syndrome, Lucius remains a cool man-about-town, always ready to jump into his Supersuit to save the day.

The Super Years

Frozone was sophisticated and cool at the height of the Supers' glory days. As one of the best Supers around, he was also adored by the ladies.

CONFIDENTIAL

The Undercover Years

Lucius would be fine if it weren't for his best friend, Bob. These two have been spotted huddled in a car late at night listening to police scanners.

Boy, Frozone sure was lucky that water cooler was there!

COPY

★ CONFIDENTIAL ★

Over the years, the world has lost track of many Supers.

Every SRP agent must pledge to do his or her best to continue searching for those Supers whose whereabouts are unknown, even if all accounts lead us to believe that those Supers are no longer among the living. They risked their lives for us on a daily basis. Let's not forget about them.

COPY

MISSING

Gazerbeam

Gazerbeam (aka Simon Paladino) risked his undercover status by talking too much about Supers' rights!
—WD

SRP artist's rendition of Bob Parr's description of Gazerbeam at his resting place, the island of Nomanisan.

MISSING

Dynaguy

MISSING

Stratogale

MISSING

Thunderhead

That's me at the wedding next to E.
—R.D.

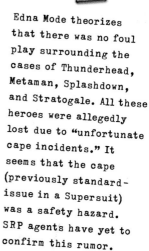

COPY

Edna Mode theorizes that there was no foul play surrounding the cases of Thunderhead, Metaman, Splashdown, and Stratogale. All these heroes were allegedly lost due to "unfortunate cape incidents." It seems that the cape (previously standard-issue in a Supersuit) was a safety hazard. SRP agents have yet to confirm this rumor.

★ CONFIDENTIAL ★

SCREECH

ALIAS: Unknown

STRENGTHS: Night vision
Flight
360° head-rotation view

WEAKNESS: May be tired and less focused during the day

Note: Screech's ability to fly is natural and not a function of his suit, which serves to give off the "Owl" vibe.

VOYD

ALIAS: Karen

STRENGTH: Dimensional teleportation

WEAKNESS: Wormhole destinations can be unpredictable.

Note: Voyd's ability to generate wormholes makes her a formidable hero perfect for missions that require long-distance travel and quick escapes.

BRICK

ALIAS: Concretia "Connie" Mason

STRENGTH: Can expand to the size and strength of a brick wall on command

WEAKNESS: Will sink in water

Note: When Brick arrives, evildoers usually find themselves between a rock and a hard place.

HE-LECTRIX

ALIAS: Unknown

STRENGTHS: Ability to control and project electric current
Impervious to electricity

WEAKNESS: Exposure to water can temporarily short out He-Lectrix's power. Also, his powers have no effect on non-conductive materials, such as wood or rubber.

Note: Any villain who encounters this high-voltage hero is in for the shock of their lives!

REFLUX

ALIAS: Gus Burns

STRENGTH: Can regurgitate his molten stomach acid

WEAKNESS: Tires easily, overheats, gets motion sickness

Note: When Reflux goes on the offensive, he is THE most offensive hero around.

KRUSHAUER

ALIAS: Unknown

STRENGTHS: Can crush objects without touching them

WEAKNESS: Can only crush inanimate objects

Note: When Krushauer battles the bad guys, he never fails to leave a lasting impression and a trail of rubble in his wake.

From: Winston
To: Evelyn

Subject: New Faces

Good thought. If they play well with others, maybe we can assemble a Superhero team . . . this time, one that isn't related.

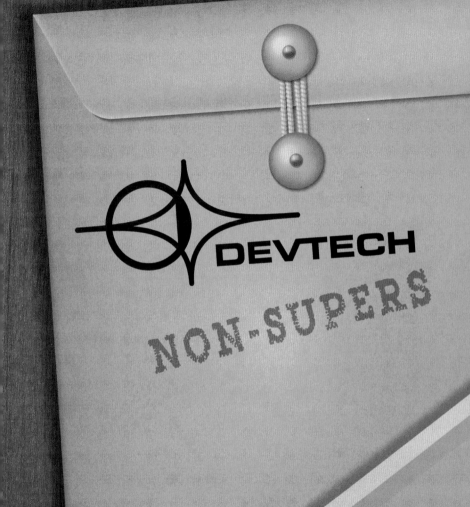

From: Winston

To: Evelyn

Subject: Non-Super Individuals

Everybody needs friends, and Supers are no exception. Especially when you're trying to improve their image.

Along with sidekicks and Super allies, let's not forget the non-super individuals (NSIs). From the plucky reporters to stalwart law-enforcement officials, these ordinary folks have an extraordinary impact on justice. Let's start an NSI dossier.

Already started.
Below are some
of the first profiles.
—ED

RICK DICKER

ional Commendation

NOTE: Rick Dicker was appointed Agent in Charge of the Super Relocation Program. After the Sansweet Incident, in which Mr. Incredible was charged with endangering the life of a despondent citizen, the Supers were forced into retirement. Supers attempting to fit in sometimes learned that X-ray vision or Super strength couldn't fix every problem. That's where Rick came in. When needed, he helped Supers find new places to live and establish new secret identities.

For years, Rick was the most unflappable ally a Super could have, keeping them as well as the general populace safe. Rick's steady temperament helped defuse situations more volatile than one of Bomb Voyage's grenades.

Besides being a great mentor during my time at the SKP, Rick personally oversaw every case involving Supers and the public, conducting each interview himself. In fact, he became the face of the SKP—that is, until the Mindwipe was invented (see Gadgets). Now most people who encounter Rick never remember it.

—WD

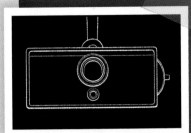

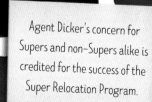

Agent Dicker's concern for Supers and non-Supers alike is credited for the success of the Super Relocation Program.

NOTE:

One name towers above all others in the world of fashion: Edna Mode, the czarina of the catwalk, the minuscule maven of Milan. Yet while her work with supermodels is well-known, her work with the Supers remains among her best.

Taking the Supers out of circulation took the starch out of Edna's career as a Super designer. But like her signature haluminum vibronic dacralor polymesh (patent pending), she soon snapped back. Rumors suggested that she stayed in contact with many Supers, even doing occasional alterations for them.

COUTURE CRAZE DAILY

YOUR GUIDE TO HAUTE COUTURE FROM THE RUNWAYS OF THE WORLD

THIS FALL EVERYONE WILL BE WEARING BULLETPROOF!

THE SPANDEX ISSUE

FEATURING SUPER-SUIT EXTRAORDINAIRE, E!

SUPERHERO STYLE meets HIGH FASHION this fall!

When Edna abandoned capes in her designs, the fashion world couldn't wrap their head around it. They had no idea that the lack of capes originated in her super-secret Super designs. But in time, they came around to her way of thinking, proving once again that looking back only "distracts from the now, *dahling.*"

Contact E.M.

Subject: Designing T-shirts and a clothing line for non-Supers. Good deeds will need a good look.

—WD

E

E
at the height
of fashion fame

EDNA MODE

Identity:
Edna Mode

Occupation:
Fashion designer

Greatest achievements:
"Everything I do is perfect, *dahling.*"

Best known for:
Supersuit designs

Current projects:
Redesigning haluminum vibronic dacralor polymesh

The Undercover Years

Edna Mode, renowned designer to the Supers, has not been spotted in their presence in years. We suspect that she has little, if any, influence on the Supers.

To my dahling,
i simply did not have time to create this Supersuit for you. (But i did it anyway. Call it insanity!) You look fabulous!
xxxooo Edna Mode

A Super New Era

Memo to file:
Now that the Supers are back
doing hero work, will we be
hearing and seeing much more
of Edna Mode? She recently
canceled her spring show
in Milan. Is she designing
exclusively for Supers now?
(I must say, her Supersuit
designs are quite astounding,
and nearly indestructible.)

E was in contact with
Mr. Incredible when
he first returned to
hero work.

Survived volcanic eruption.
Do not use bleach.
—Edna Mode

Worth watching. If we
know what Ms. Mode is
doing, we are likely to know
what the Supers are doing.
—ED

Subject: Edna Mode

A reclusive fashion designer, her appreciation for privacy has made her a trusted tailor to Supers for years. Plus her sense of style is practically a Super power.

Edna operates exclusively from an ultra-secure studio in the basement of her estate on the outskirts of Municiberg. From there she has everything she needs to design and create the most fashion-forward yet functional herowear. Not surprising, given Mode's philosophy: Luck favors the prepared.

Edna's design studio rivals ours here at DevTech!

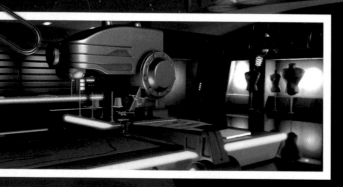

From: Winston

To: Evelyn

Subject: Super Villains

Bringing the Supers back into the light will require some dark characters. I'm talking Super villains. Like regular villains, but with something extra. With Syndrome gone and the Underminer's whereabouts unknown, we need to find the perfect bad guy.

From: Evelyn
To: Winston

NOT FOR CIRCULATION

The current crop of villains is lacking. Most have gone underground, just like the Supers. Those we have located are quietly pursuing "legit" lines of work.

Their egos are often their downfall—they love to reveal their plans!

If only they'd stop monologuing!
—ED

Our man in Paris thinks he's located Bomb Voyage working as a street mime, but I think that's a little hard to swallow.

Yeah, if I were working as a mime, I'd keep quiet about it, too!
—WD

SYNDROME

Poster image found on Nomanisan. This guy loved being bad.

CONFIDENTIAL

Former name:
Buddy

Super powers:
None

Former claim to fame:
President of Mr. Incredible's fan club

Fatal flaw:
Overestimating technology

Greatest achievement:
Creating the Omnidroid

COPY

Syndrome went through 9 prototype Omnidroids before launching his ultimate invention on the city.
—ED

The Golden Age

Buddy was Mr. Incredible's biggest fan. Then one day, Mr. Incredible told him to go home—he simply was not a Super and never would be. The rest is history. Buddy became one of the greatest enemies of the Supers.

Fan club disbanded

Cape led to downfall

The Undercover Years

COPY

SUBJECT TERMINATED

WARNING

Syndrome could be the number-one worst villain of all time!

SURVEILLANCE PHOTO

CONFIDENTIAL

A Super New Era

UPDATE: Syndrome is no longer a threat to Supers or to Metroville, thanks to the Incredibles and Frozone. We mourn the loss of those Supers destroyed by this nefarious villain.

MIRAGE

★ CONFIDENTIAL ★

COPY

NOT BREAK SEAL **EVIDENCE** DO NOT BREAK SEAL **EVIDENCE** DO NOT BREAK

Real name:
Unknown

Occupation:
Syndrome's
assistant

Bad deed:
Lured Mr. Incredible
to work for Syndrome

Good deed:
Betrayed Syndrome
and saved
Mr. Incredible

**Current
whereabouts:**
Unknown

Status:
Keep this file
RED HOT. Mirage
could surface
anywhere at any
time—either as
friend or foe.

Mirage is very good
at undercover work.
She can skip off our
radar within minutes.

EVIDENCE

Name:	Mirage
Content:	Mini microphone
Location:	Front seat of car
Time:	11:46 p.m.
SRP Agent:	R. Dicker
Page Number:	34

When Mirage worked for Syndrome, she did spectacular spy work. The SRP didn't even know she existed. Mirage was actually targeting Lucius when she found Bob. Targets were quickly switched.

★ CONFIDENTIAL ★

Photo confiscated from Syndrome's headquarters. It was taken by a surveillance camera in Mirage's car.

Run tests on photo to see what Mirage would look like with different hair color, etc.

Current Info

REPORT: Incredibles escape Syndrome with assistance

NAME: Mirage

ORIGIN: Still unknown

MISSION: Still unknown

LAST SEEN: On the island of Nomanisan; is she in contact with the Parrs?

Received a tip that Mirage has recently been spotted with an unnamed Super.

Mirage has a talent with computer systems.
—ED

From: Evelyn
To: Winston

Subject: Super Villain Report

May have found the ideal candidate. Reports of a brilliant, mysterious tech villain named the Screenslaver.

Word on the street is the Screenslaver is a computer and engineering genius. They say there's not a system he can't hack. Including biologicals. Possible mind control? Given his advanced computer skills, the Screenslaver may not even be human, but rather some form of living AI?

Two bonuses: No cape and lets the crime do the talking (no monologuing!!).
—ED

From: Winston
To: Evelyn

Subject: Super Villains

Wow, very in-depth intel! Keep me posted on possible high-value targets and the Screenslaver's next moves. And do we like that name, the Screenslaver? Did he come up with that himself? Maybe we can think of something with more punch.

From: Evelyn
To: Winston

Subject: Super Villain Report

Targets that are as high-tech as they are high-profile are the most likely places for someone as brilliant as the Screenslaver to strike. I suggest looking at the MetroLev unveiling, for starters. (See Vehicles.)

P.S. Actually, the Screenslaver is a pretty impressive name. It's a pun and a mashup, which indicates very high-level thinking. I think the Screenslaver will be a formidable adversary.
—ED

THE INCREDIBILE

The Most "Super" Vehicle Ever?

SPEC SHEET

Top Speed:	300 mph (estimated)
	100 knots (hydro mode)
	0-60: 3.0 seconds/1.5 with turbine
Engine:	Jet turbine
Features:	Turbo boost
	Manual/autodrive
	Ejector seats
	Remote operation
	Crime Tracker 4000 onboard computer
	Auto-costume feature/suit loading

Eliminating the need
for a second car,
the Incredibile can
operate in sedan or
stealth mode and
appear as an ordinary,
late-model sedan when
the Incredibles aren't
fighting crime. But
with the press of a
button, it transforms
into Super mode to
become the scourge
of evildoers.

The Many Modes
of the Incredibile

Hydro
In this mode, the Incredibile is capable of traveling on water.

Hover Autodrive
This is the ultimate cruise control. Once in autodrive mode, the Incredibile's onboard computer handles all navigation, pursuit, and anti-collision duties, leaving the driver free to change, take a quick shave, or finish a bite on the go.

Intercept
GPS meets "Gee whiz!" The Incredibile's Intercept mode tracks not only a criminal's route—but also all vehicles in pursuit. It projects and plots the most effective intercept course. This maximizes Mr. Incredible's crime-fighting time, as well as his mpg!

Juke
The Incredibile's AI-enhanced avoidance system means it can detect and evade threats and obstacles even faster than most Supers. This leaves Mr. Incredible free to focus on the pursuit instead of potential collateral damage.

And moving violations, increased insurance rates, lawsuits. —ED

Why reinvent the wheel? Let's just buy the original Incredibile back. Check car collectors, junk yards, call the Frederickson Auto Museum! Also, what's the status of the Elasticycle?
—WD

From: Evelyn
To: Winston

Subject: The Elasticycle

A good Super vehicle reflects its hero, and the Elasticycle is no exception. With the ability to split in two, the redesigned Elasticycle stretches more than gas mileage—it lets Elastigirl use her remarkable stretching powers even at top speed. It's also available in both a gas and an electric model.

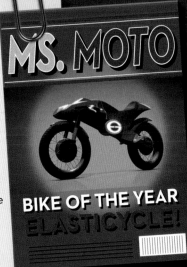

MS. MOTO

BIKE OF THE YEAR
ELASTICYCLE!

SPEC SHEET

Top speed:	200 mph (0–60 in 2.3 seconds)
Capacity:	1043 cc
Bore/Stroke in.:	77/56
Output:	140 bhp @ 9,600 rpm
Torque:	82 lbs./ft. @ 8,800 rpm
Type:	4-stroke, 4-cyclinder, DOHC, 16-valve, liquid-cooled
Transmission:	6-speed

* Twin fuel cells by DevTech power the EC. Having one of these state-of-the-art engines in each half of the bike means that whether stretched out or not, it's still one of the fastest vehicles on two wheels.

* The fuel cells are a solar-hydrogen hybrid design. The only emission is water. The "no footprint" feature makes it good for the environment and good for missions where stealth is important.

* Tires from the DevTech Advanced Polymerics division. The DAP polysynthetic, or Devomer (patent pending), is designed to resist punctures.

* Solid rubber means no need to inflate.

From: Evelyn
To: Winston

Subject: Tunneler

Our engineers dug up the following dirt on the Underminer's tunneler after the Omnidroid incident last year. Absolutely the wrong vehicle choice for a hero concerned about his or her reputation. However, it is an impressive machine. One of the largest vehicles on the planet (or under it), the tunneler has a reinforced titanium hull and is powered by a trio of 3,500 hp diesel engines and a pair of hydraulic engines that turn the tunneler's massive diamond-tipped, ultranium-carbide drill. It can cut through the hardest rock or steel . . . and remain razor-sharp! It may not be much to look at, but this villainous vehicle can withstand—and drill through—any environment.

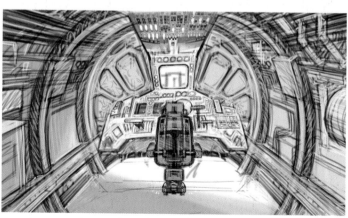

From the command center, the Underminer can travel through any surface on Earth with the tunneler's massive drill. It's big, powerful, and simple—it only has two gears: clockwise and counterclockwise. But when you generate almost 300,000 ft./lbs. of torque, you don't need anything else.

Additional Features

The tunneler isn't long on extras, but it comes equipped with a powerful vacuum generator, which the Underminer can use to extract objects. The generator can be reversed to pump out objects as well. And when it does, it really blows! It also includes an escape drill, should the need arise.

SPEC SHEET

POWER

Main engine:	3x3,500 horsepower diesel engines
Drill engines:	2 hydraulic engines
Torque:	300,000 ft./lbs. max
Twin tread:	113 shoes per tread
Shoe:	500 lbs.
Curb weight:	approx. 2,000 tons

Brainstorm! The EVERJUST would make the perfect Super headquarters! Look at this thing! It's got everything!
—WD

Oh, brother. We're already giving the Incredibles a house. Now you want to provide a floating party pad to everyone in a mask or cape? I don't see why Supers should get all the cool stuff.
—ED

POSSIBLE DOCK LOCATION

From: Winston

To: Evelyn

Subject: Possible Super vehicles . . . an Incredi-copter?

Attached is information about the ambassadors' helicopters for reference. Their vertical takeoff capability is advantageous, and their speed makes them useful for transporting a hero or a team of heroes to danger zones quickly. Spacious seating also comes in handy for rescue operations.

Helicopters

Note: Helen Parr is a licensed pilot.
—WD

COUNTERMEASURES

Flares: Heat-seeking missiles

Chaff: Heat-seeking and guided missiles, Air-to-Air (ATA) missiles, radar resistant fuselage, various scanning systems, electronic jamming system

Infrared jamming system: Heat-seeking missiles

SPEC SHEET

Max speed: 250 knots (with jet turbo)
Fuselage: Reinforced composite fiber
Capacity: 3 cockpit, 6 cabin

FEATURES

9 safety/emergency kits, including
parachutes and glide suits
Retractable landing gear
Auxiliary jet turbine

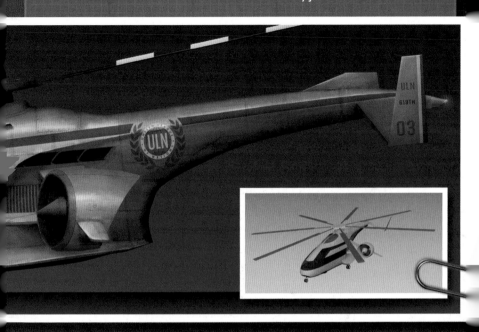

Monorail

The Municiberg Monorail is the pride of
the city. Quick and dependable, this mass-
transit system can take you practically
anywhere in Municiberg in minutes.
With advances in public transportation,
such as the MetroLev (see next page) and
repeated Super villain incidents, fewer
commuters rely on the monorail. Still, it
remains an affordable way to travel and
to see the sights of Municiberg.

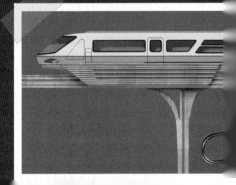

Who says public transportation has to be a drag?

New Urbem's latest technological breakthrough will revolutionize how (and how fast) you travel! The MetroLev train uses magnets to levitate, which reduces friction and drag. This makes it extremely fast and extremely green.

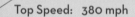

Top Speed:	380 mph
Fuel:	Superconductive magnets
Capacity:	100 passengers/car

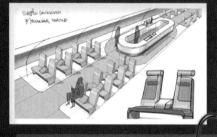

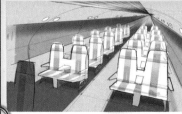

From: Winston
To: Evelyn

Subject: Super Gadgets

Our heroes need upgrades. New suits, new vehicles, new equipment. Please review and submit proposals for new Super stuff by end of the week.

W~

Here's the info you wanted for your boys in R&D. Just make sure I get this back before I leave for Bermuda.

~Rick Dicker

MW-086 DECEREBRALATOR

The official name is a mouthful, so around the SRP, we just call it the Mindwiper.

From: Evelyn
To: Winston

★ CONFIDENTIAL ★

Subject: MW-086 (The Mindwiper)

Crude but effective, the MW-086 has a variable power setting that controls how far back SRP agents can erase a person's memory. Understandably, the power to erase someone's mind would be catastrophic in the wrong hands, which is why only two of these devices were made. However, the agent responsible for the other one can't recall where she left it.

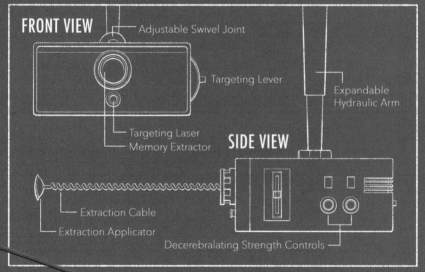

FRONT VIEW

Adjustable Swivel Joint

Targeting Lever

Expandable Hydraulic Arm

Targeting Laser
Memory Extractor

SIDE VIEW

Extraction Cable
Extraction Applicator

Decerebralating Strength Controls

MW-086 DECEREBRALATOR

(Used primarily to help keep Supers' secret identities hidden. When the SRP is repealed, the MW-086 should be repurposed or dismantled to prevent it from falling into the wrong hands.)

From: Evelyn

To: Winston

★ **CONFIDENTIAL** ★

Proof that the Screenslaver is a formidable foe comes in the form of the hypno-goggles that were confiscated from his lair. This advanced tech combines the latest in neuroscience with cameras and screens built right into the lenses.

Hypno-goggles are not only capable of delivering high-definition images—they can also project holograms, augmented reality, and virtual reality imagery. But the most astounding feature is the ability to deliver information and instructions directly into your brain.

Hypno-goggles can instantly change what you know, what you think, even what you believe!

It will change the look of crime fighting forever. The applications for the hypno-goggles are virtually limitless!

—ED

That's great! But can we do something about the look? See attached.
—WD

ediphone

Superhero means being on call.
ediphone gives us hotline access
girl and Mr. Incredible anytime,
e . . . as long as they're at home
e the ringer turned on.

ed directly to crime command
t Deavor Corporate Headquarters,
diphone is a secure line that is
ed to connect the call through
trikes, tidal waves, and more.

From: Winston

And we could call it the iPhone!

From: Deavor Legal

No. No, we cannot.

iphone also features
warding, which can route calls
the communication system
ticycle or in the Incredibile.

*Also, ringer can be set to
flash instead of ring when
Jack-Jack's down for a nap.*

—ED

Suit Cams

From: Evelyn
To: Winston

Subject: The Superhero Revolution Will Be Televised

In response to your request . . .
Media plays a critical role in the success of the Deavor
Initiative. Using images that will capture the public's
hearts and minds means getting some truly incredible
footage. Included is an example of our visitor's
suit cam (with matching lanyard), already in use
throughout the company.

Suit cams by DevTech allow us to make big
news out of even the smallest good deeds.

With miniaturization technology, we can
embed cameras in badges, buttons, and pins—
then stream the footage in real time.

Signal Tracker

The Signal Tracker can detect all known radio and television signals.

The Signal Tracker is also the latest in anti-espionage technology. It can sweep a room for bugging devices and disable them with a small EMP burst.

SIGNAL ACQUIRED

The Signal Tracker readout includes a GPS, which makes it easy to find the source of transmissions within a 100-mile radius and plot the quickest intercept course.

ISOLATE PURSUIT

From: Evelyn
To: Winston

Subject: The Jack-Jack Tracker

Now that Jack-Jack is a Super (and a polymorph), this gadget will prove the most important in the entire Incredible arsenal.

Developed by Edna Mode, this amazing device has almost as many functions as Jack-Jack! The intuitive interface lets anyone monitor Jack-Jack's mood and track and record new powers that appear, and most important, it stores a playlist of songs arranged specifically to keep him from melting down.

...racker also features the
...Num and nappy monitors,
...track the supply of cookies
...iapers and automatically
...s orders when the supply
...of either dips too low.

Also great for
babysitters!

From: Evelyn

To: Winston

Subject: Jack-Jack

Unfortunately, once Jack-Jack's powers began to manifest, no ordinary babysitter—no matter how experienced—was a match for him.

Fortunately, Edna Mode is no ordinary babysitter. She keeps her cool no matter what form Jack-Jack takes.

REPLICATION EVENT
00:03

The Jack-Jack Tracker's Duraplex glass screen withstands heat, cold, smudging, and teething.

From: Winston
To: Evelyn

Subject: Super Lair

We can't keep the Incredibles in the Safari Court forever. A Superhero family needs a super place to live. I had people look into the old Syndrome lair on Nomanisan Island, but it's being turned into a theme park and resort—like the world needs another one of those!

Unfortunately, there are no realtors in Municiberg who handle clients like ours. Ideas?

The Island was impractical anyway. How about a solution a little closer to home—one of our homes?

—ED

Perfect! It's secluded, with a commanding view and plenty of room for the whole Parr family. Let's get our people on it to make the necessary renovations for the vehicles. We'll also need to Super-baby-proof the place! The lower level makes the perfect hangar deck for flying Supers and their vehicles. The disappearing pool provides the perfect cover.

—WD

From: Winston

Replace all windows with Impervium bullet-proof glass. Reinforce the foundations to withstand earthquakes, meteor strikes, and Jack-Jack meltdowns.

In civilian mode, the backyard pool area and Grand Room are ideal places for the Parrs to unwind and entertain. Both pools can be hidden, if necessary.

Front elevation of the Parr Home. The standard in crime-fighting curb appeal.